THIS BOOK BELONGS TO:

_____

⚜

To Margie, my queen,
and Cooper, Chloe, and Samson
the court jesters

Visit us at shadowmountain.com

Library of Congress Cataloging-in-Publication Data

Fullmer, Howard, 1968-
  The king's highway / Howard Fullmer.
    p. cm.
  Summary: When the king announces that whoever travels his highway the best will be the next king, a young shepherd boy learns that he does not have to be of noble blood to perform noble acts and possess noble virtues.
  ISBN-10   1-59038-631-0 (hardbound : alk. paper)
  ISBN-13   978-1-59038-631-6 (hardbound : alk. paper)
  [1. Folklore.]   I. Title.
PZ8.1.F95923Ki 2006
[E]—dc22   2006008568

Printed in the United States of America
Inland Press, Menomonee Falls, WI

10   9   8   7   6   5   4   3   2   1

THE KING'S HIGHWAY

Retold and Illustrated by

HOWARD FULLMER

SHADOW
MOUNTAIN

nce there was a wise

king who had no family.

he king grew old and, knowing he had no successor, proclaimed that in three days' time he would hold a contest and whoever best traveled his highway to the castle would be crowned the new king.

The decree was read throughout the land. On the morning of the third day, spectators lined the road to watch as those who wished to be king began their travels.

tanding at the road's edge, a young shepherd named Michael tended his flock. Gazing at the crowds, he asked, "Why has everyone gathered on the king's highway?"

"Haven't you heard?" replied a stranger. "Today the highway's best traveler will become the new king."

ach traveler was dressed in his finest clothing. The Knight rode a magnificent horse. Never had Michael seen such a splendid display. Wondering which traveler would be chosen, he gathered his sack of bread and cheese and followed the grand parade.

he group trekked on, each hoping to be judged the best traveler.

Just as the castle came into view, the travelers discovered a mound of rubble blocking the highway.

"How can we travel with this in our way?" they cried.

"My fine clothing shall get dirty," said one.

"I would have to come down from my horse," said the noble knight.

"My many servants could clear this, but they are home guarding my wealth," said the rich merchant.

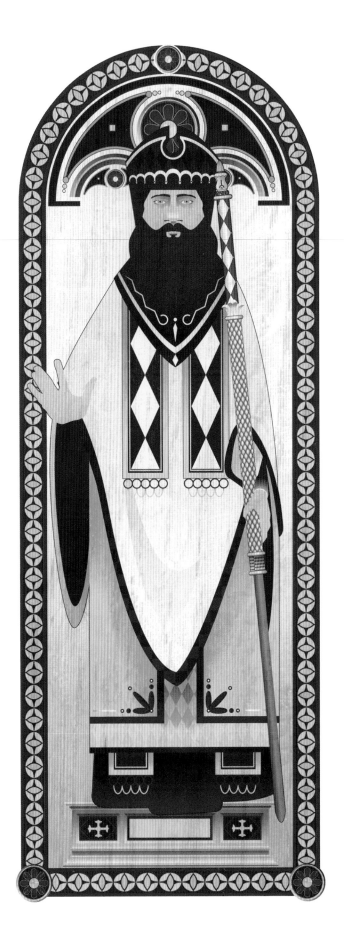

nowing that someone there would be the new king, Michael worked his way through the crowd and started clearing the rubble so each could continue. He opened a narrow path for the rich merchant to pass. He continued until there was space for the knight on his horse to get through. He kept working and smiled at each traveler until all had passed. By then the sun was low and just a few stones remained.

ending to pick up another rock, Michael noticed something sparkling in the soil. He brushed the dust away to reveal a golden ring bearing the royal crest. "This is the king's," he said. "Someone should return it." He looked around, but the parade had long since passed, and no one remained to carry the ring.

mptying his bundle of
bread and cheese, he
carefully wrapped the ring in the cloth.
Then, with the stars beginning to dance in
the sky, Michael cupped the priceless
package in his hands and raced alone
down the highway toward the castle.

As the travelers were celebrating their arrival, Michael finally reached the castle. The king, standing near the courtyard gate, looked at the boy. "It is nearly night, my son," he said, smiling for the first time that evening. "What has kept you?"

 am sorry it is so late, Your Majesty," whispered Michael, his voice trembling. "I found this while traveling. No one was left to return it so I have come." Then, carefully unwrapping his bundle, he revealed the king's ring for all to see.

Taking the ring in his hand, the wise king looked first at it, then at Michael. "This ring is not mine," he said.

"But it must be yours, Your Majesty," said the boy. "It bears your crest."

es, it does bear the crest of royalty," said the king, "but the ring now belongs to you. I proclaimed that he who best traveled the highway would become the new king. By clearing the road so that all could travel, you showed that it is not fine clothing, fancy horses, or even great wealth that make a king. It is by serving others that one becomes great.

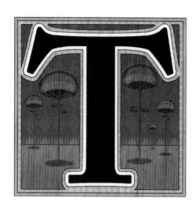oday, my son, you best traveled my highway."

Then, sliding the ring onto the boy's finger, the king proclaimed Michael the new ruler of the land.